CIAO, SANDRO!

words by
Steven Varni

pictures by
Luciano Lozano

ABRAMS BOOKS FOR YOUNG READERS
NEW YORK

Nicola was a gondolier,
like his father and
grandfather before him.

And Sandro was his
constant companion.

Ever since Nicola had found him as a puppy, they'd gone everywhere together. Sandro was Nic's loyal first mate, navigator, and guard dog whenever Nic was called away from the boat.

On warm days when they didn't have passengers, Nic and Sandro would catnap together in the sun.

And in the winter, Nic made a little bed, where Sandro was rocked to sleep by gentle waves and the soft lullaby of his best friend's oar moving through the water.

Today Nic seated two passengers in the gondola, just like any other day. But today, Sandro had no time to nap. He had people to see, places to go!

"Need a break, Sandro? Go for a stroll. You know the city better than I do now. I'll see you here later."

Off Sandro went, his tail high, proud to be taking his first walk alone. He was on an important—and secret—mission!

The calli were crammed with tourists. Sandro saw before him a forest of slow-moving legs and feet. He dodged an overloaded delivery cart to his right, a clattering suitcase to his left. Then he darted into one of the narrowest alleys in the city, which tourists never noticed and where delivery carts couldn't fit.

Like all real Venetians, Sandro knew every shortcut in their old maze of a city.

Like them, Sandro used his nose to tell the wind's direction by whether it smelled fresh and salty like the sea or muddy and weedy like the lagoon.

Like them, his ears remembered how a vaporetto growled and spluttered every time it slowed for its next stop, like a grumpy sea monster getting out of bed.

And his paws knew exactly how the ancient mosaic floor in the Basilica di San Marco dipped and swelled like the sea itself.

But Sandro knew these things even *better* than most Venetians, because he had a dog's extra-sensitive nose and ears. In fact . . .

it was his nose that detected the first hint of
Alvise's espurgopozzineri boat, and he followed
its unmistakable odor straight to his friend.

"CIAO, SANDRO!"

Alvise called out. He was used to always seeing
Sandro with Nicola, so he asked, "To what do I
owe this special visit, mio caro?"

Sandro wagged his tail in reply and gave Alvise
time to think about it.

"Ah, I understand . . . Don't worry, Sandro, I
haven't forgotten."

That's just what Sandro wanted to hear! With
a fond lick of Alvise's hand, off he went.

Francesca also worked from a boat, selling fruits and vegetables. Hers was usually docked in the same place. Today Sandro heard the sweet sound of Francesca humming to herself from far off, and he followed his ears.

"CIAO, SANDRO!"

She quickly clambered ashore to scoop him up into a hug.

"What do you think of these beauties?
You think our friend will like them?"

Sandro sniffed every single one of them,
then wagged his tail in approval.

"I think he will, too!"

Then Sandro set off again.
Next stop: Murano!

Sandro's paws knew the feel of the city so well he could have crossed it in his sleep.

They carried him over the splintery planks of the Accademia Bridge;

across warm paving stones of grand campi;

up and down steps of
iron, concrete, and
marble worn smooth
by centuries of feet;

all the way to the
vaporetto stop.

Sandro knew exactly which vaporetto to board.

But a marinaio noticed Sandro waiting alone outside the steering cabin as the boat got underway. He picked him up and carried him among the passengers, seeking out his owner.

When no one claimed him, he brought Sandro to Captain Tiozzo.

"CIAO, SANDRO!"

she exclaimed.

"You *know* this lost dog?" the surprised marinaio asked.

"Certo!" she said. "And I promise you, Jacopo, this smart little guy is not lost. He always rides this line with his owner, my friend Nicola. Put him down and watch. He's sure to get off at the second stop."

Jacopo looked doubtful, but he set Sandro down, and soon the little dog's nose twitched at a scent of molten glass that neither person could smell. At the second stop he got off, just as Captain Tiozzo had said he would!

Inside the shadowy vetreria, Sandro kept far away from the red-hot blobs of glass that Giorgio and his three sons were shaping. And from the furnaces, too, which burned at a temperature of 2,967 degrees Fahrenheit—hotter than lava from a volcano!

He barked a greeting.

"CIAO, SANDRO!"

"Can you keep a secret?" Giorgio asked, and he showed Sandro the most beautiful goblet. "We all worked on it," he said proudly. Sandro sniffed the goblet, then gave it the gentlest of admiring licks.

"Grazie!" Giorgio said. "I'm so happy you like it!"

Then he offered Sandro a snack. But now Sandro's mission was complete, and he was eager to get back to Nicola. He headed for the door.

Sandro hurried back to Venice.

"CIAO,

When Sandro arrived at the gondola at last, Nicola scratched him behind his ears in just the right spot. "Did you have an adventurous afternoon?" Nic asked. Sandro answered with licks and a wagging tail.

Then Sandro and Nicola set off with one last boatload of passengers, just like any other day.

After the ride, they walked home together
to their family, just like any other day.

But Sandro had known all day long that this was not just like any other day.

And he'd spent the afternoon making sure that none of their friends had forgotten it, either.

SURPRISE!

GLOSSARY

(and pronunciation)

a dopo (*ah DOH-poh*): see you later

buon compleanno (*bwohn cohm-pleh-AHN-noh*): happy birthday

calli (*CALL-lee*) (singular: **calle**; *CALL-lay*): narrow streets, alleys

campi (*CAHM-pee*) (singular: **campo**; *CAHM-poh*): In Venice, this means "paved squares or plazas"; in the rest of Italy, it means "open fields." Venice's campi were once open fields too, but they have been paved for a long time.

certo (*CHER-toh*): certainly, of course

ciao (*chow*): Means both "hello" and "good-bye"

espurgopozzineri (*ay-SPOOR-goh-POHTS-zee-NAY-ree*): A tanker boat that collects toilet waste flushed into septic tanks, which are hidden in the ground floors of some Venetian buildings. But most toilets and sinks in Venice still empty into the canals, as they have for centuries, to be carried out to sea twice a day by the tide.

gondola (*GOHN-doh-lah*): The most famous kind of traditional flat-bottomed boat in Venice. It is 35.5 feet long and 4.5 feet at its widest point, and weighs about 850 pounds. For many centuries they were used like limousines by wealthy Venetians and like taxis by everyone else, but for the last hundred years they have been the favorite ride of tourists!

grazie (*GRAH-zee-ay*): thank you

marinaio (*mah-ree-NYE-yoh*): sailor. Each vaporetto is staffed by one marinaio and one captain.

mio caro (*ME-oh CAH-roh*) (feminine form: **mia cara**; *ME-ah CAH-rah*): my dear friend

vaporetto (*vah-poh-RHET-toh*) (plural: **vaporetti**; *vah-poh-RHET-tee*): waterbus. There are no streets or cars in Venice, only canals, so vaporetti are the city's only public transportation system. They follow their routes around the city and the lagoon and make regular stops, just like buses do on land.

vetreria (*veh-tray-REE-ah*): glassblowing factory

For Jen and Alessandro
—S. V.
To Lola and Bobby
—L. L.

The illustrations in this book were made with watercolor pencils, India ink, and most of all, with an iPad Pro.

Library of Congress Cataloging-in-Publication Data has been applied for and may be obtained from the Library of Congress.

ISBN 978-1-4197-4390-0

Text copyright © 2021 Steven Varni
Illustrations copyright © 2021 Luciano Lozano
Book design by Heather Kelly

Printed and bound in China
10 9 8 7 6 5 4 3 2 1

Abrams Books for Young Readers are available at special discounts when purchased in quantity for premiums and promotions as well as fundraising or educational use. Special editions can also be created to specification. For details, contact specialsales@abramsbooks.com or the address below.

Abrams® is a registered trademark of Harry N. Abrams, Inc.

ABRAMS The Art of Books
195 Broadway, New York, NY 10007
abramsbooks.com

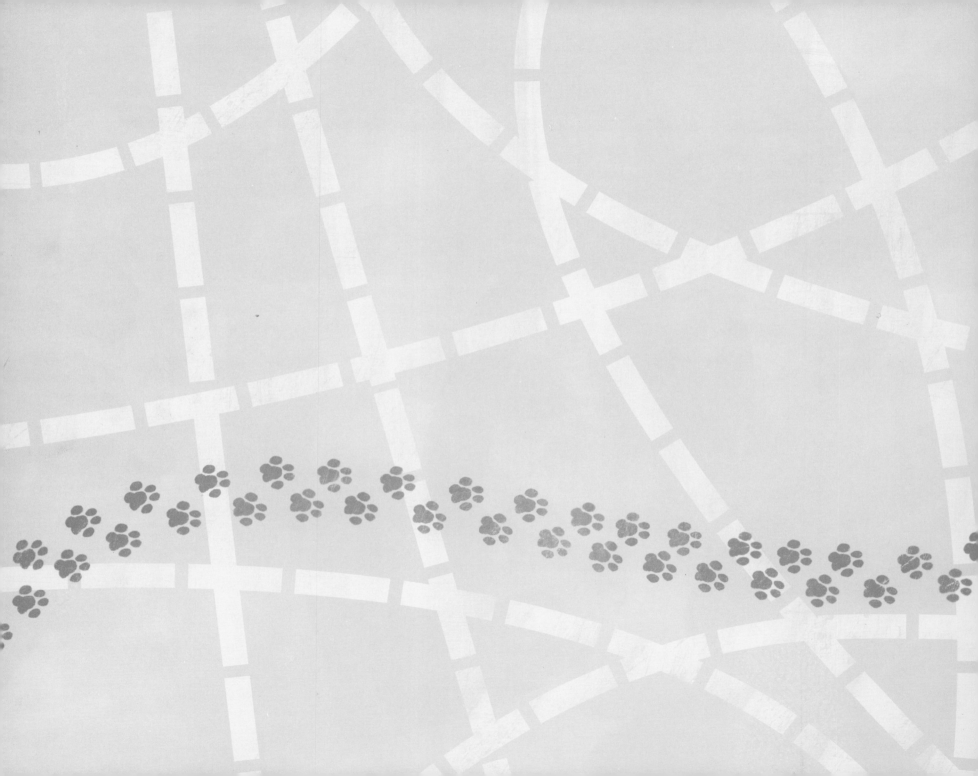